Age of Humanity:

# Born Hunter

Dave Rudden

ISBN: 1492867373
ISBN-13: 978-1492867371

# DEDICATION

To those who have inspired me in my writing. First, there are my fellow students in my college creative writing class, who said my story of a sniper on a lone mission sounded more like a novel than a short story. At the time, I disregarded their comments, never thinking I would actually write anything. Now, their comments carry me.

Then came my sister-in-law, who was the first to listen to me ramble on about a story idea, and who inspired me to develop my story ideas until I had an entire world developed in my head. It took me a long time to get all the story points ready, but as I start to publish my books, I think back to that day so many years ago.

When I started this journey as a writer, I ran into problems, along with rewrites and more rewrites. It took me two years to write my first novel, only to get rejection letters from tons of agents. I decided to write five shorter stories (this is the first of the five) to try my hand at self-publishing. The decision to self-publish led to the unique experience of being interviewed by another aspiring writer named Ian Foster.

Ian is a young boy who read a book and then said he wanted to be an author. A single book changed Ian's life, and he changed mine. To look at him, you would not know he is autistic. When his teacher, Mrs. Phillips, told me what to expect during the interview, I had no idea what I was getting into. Until that interview, the only experience I'd had with autism was watching what my friends went through with their severely autistic son.

After talking to Ian and then learning about his struggles, I realized that no matter what struggles I face, whether massive rewrites or horrible reviews, I can do this. Because of this boy, I am going to write my story down and push through the hard times. I recognize how this young man, who struggled to read and write and even speak, now wants to dominate the enemy he's battled for so long, and write a book. Maybe one day someone will read one of my stories and get inspired in the same way.

Thank you, Mrs. Phillips, for the opportunity to meet Ian. Thank you, Ian, for being who you are. I can't wait to put your first book on the shelf next to mine.

# CONTENTS

# ACKNOWLEDGMENTS

Special thanks go to me team

Kristy – Proof reader and critic

Phil Moreshed – Proof Reader and soundboard for story ideas

John Patten – Cover artist

Lynda Dietz – Editor. Follow her on Easy Reader
http://ilovetoreadyourbooks.blogspot.com/

# 1
# BIRTHRIGHT

Andrew Singer stood over the open wooden chest that sat next to his bed in the back of his small bedroom. The bed was made with military corners so tight they would put some soldiers' efforts to shame. He secured his holster to his right hip and adjusted its placement until it was sitting right where he wanted. He placed two extra magazines for his 9mm Beretta in the left cargo pocket of his camouflage military fatigues and loaded a third into the pistol before securing it in the holster.

Drew stood just under 5'9" with a muscular build. His light brown hair was cut short enough to pass military inspection. He didn't look like the typical eighteen-year-old kid bursting with dreams of heading off to college or finding a girl to take to the movies. Any thought of childhood innocence had been replaced with the hard realities of life; he knew war and death and it showed in the cold look in his eyes.

"Are you ready?" His father spoke from the doorway behind him.

Dan Singer had a similar build to his son, but stood 6'2" with longer blond hair, and his facial hair was just starting to show a few days of growth.

"Just about," Drew replied as he placed a tan armored vest over his head. "I want to do one more gear check."

"Lay it out for me again."

"Do you want the mission or the plan?"

"Both." Dan walked into the room and stood near a small wooden desk that was against the wall.

Drew presented the information as if he were an instructor in front of one of his many tactics classes. He had been studying tactics ever since he was nine, and had a natural talent for laying out plans. This wasn't his first mission, but it was the first time he had been able to take part in the planning. "Two days ago, a couple coming home from a party found an abandoned car on Route 10 outside of Melville, Louisiana. The car's front end was smashed, and there was no sign of the driver or what the car had hit. Local police found traces of fur in the car's grill and they suspected the driver hit a large deer and got lost going for help. When a fifty-mile search of the area was conducted, we found a large number of people had gone missing in the last two months. Our intelligence unit expanded their search and found that all the missing people had been taken within fifty miles from a nearby town called Mamou, Louisiana, but no one has been reported missing from the town itself."

Drew pulled out a map from the cargo pocket of his pants and laid it out on the desk.

"The attack near Melville is just latest attack within the fifty-mile radius. With the fur and the short distance, we suspect we're looking for a werewolf living somewhere in Mamou," he said, pointing to the map.

In most families, mentioning a werewolf would get you a trip to the doctor to get your head examined, but werewolves, vampires, witches and all sorts of demons were discussed freely in the Singer family. They talked about each creature's strengths, weakness and most importantly how to hunt and kill each type of nightmarish monster. The Singers, and the nearly hundred other families that were part of their organization, dedicated their lives to hunting monsters, and keeping the rest of the world from ever finding out the nightmares were real.

"What's the plan?" Dan asked his son.

"Mamou is a mining town. The intelligence unit is going in as potential investors as their cover. They're looking for a local who has become detached within the last six months. The roads and hiking paths outside town will be watched for any activity while they conduct their investigation."

"Why do you assume it's a local? Why aren't you looking for a newcomer in town?" Dan asked, interrupting his son.

"Because no one is missing from town. A newcomer wouldn't care if people in town disappeared. We're looking for someone who cares enough about the town to leave it alone. The werewolf is most likely a likeable person with no enemies in town. If it had any enemies, the beast would have killed them by now."

"What's the plan when you find the werewolf?"

"We'll eliminate it. We hope to make it look like it's just another one of the missing people; that way we can avoid any press or scandal."

"What about closure for the families of the missing people?"

"Unfortunately, we need to remain hidden. In order to avoid any press, we'll have to avoid a direct attack or admitting we're there to hunt a killer.

The families will have to continue to think their loved ones are missing. Unless we find the bodies."

"What will you do then?"

"It depends on how the situation plays out. We'll alert the authorities to the bodies and can claim the werewolf was either the serial killer or one of the victims."

"Very good, son. It sounds like you've thought of everything," Dan said, giving his son a hug. "Good luck. Come back in one piece or your mother will kill me."

"Trust your men, Dad. They're good at what they do. You trained them, after all."

# 2
# FIRST MISSION

Drew took his assignment seriously, but sitting in a jeep ten miles out of town was as boring as it sounds. He tried to pass the time by studying the map, but after a while, he had memorized every part of it.

"Keep staring at that map, and you're going to burn a hole in it," Jason Riley said from the driver's seat.

Jason had spent ten years in the Army's Special Forces, including two tours in Vietnam, before running into a pack of zombies in the Mekong Delta. The way he'd handled the situation had earned him a position as a hunter. Now he was the team leader of one of the two hunting teams in the organization, with Drew's father leading the second team.

"Sorry," Drew said. "I'm just trying to stay focused."

"Keep your mind clear, and focus on the job. Study the road and take in the details. If you're busy looking at the map, your reaction time will be slowed down when trouble hits."

"Aren't you bored?"

"Boredom is the part of the job, but so is discipline. Run different scenarios through your head. Try to imagine all the different ways thing could happen, then figure out how you'd react. It'll keep you sharp and alert. Plus, if things do go sideways, you'll already have planned out different ways to deal with the situation. "

For the next few days, Drew and Jason rotated shifts with another team. To pass the time, Jason would tell war stories or quiz Drew on tactics. When they weren't on duty, they would catch some sleep at the base camp a few miles away or go over possible strategies if they had to take the town.

During their shifts, the units stayed hidden and off the road, documenting every vehicle coming and going. If the werewolf "made" the intelligence unit in town and tried to escape, the tactical unit would at least have a record of the vehicles and an idea of where to start hunting.

On the third day, the intelligence unit called to report in with the tactical unit. Jason took the call and put it on speaker so Drew could hear the conversation.

"We believe we've found our suspect." Drew didn't recognize the female voice on the other end of the phone.

"There's a young woman named Kathleen Dustin. She's a waitress at a small diner called Franky's. Recently she's been letting her hair and nails grow out. According to our sources, she used to take care of herself, and would get all made up before coming to work. Now she looks like she rolled out of bed. She also doesn't seem to have any friends. All she does is go to work and return home to a small house at the edge of town."

"Do you have any hard evidence?" Jason asked.

"Nothing concrete, but she fits the bill of a person recently turned."

"What do you think, Drew?" Jason asked.

"We don't have enough to eliminate her. Let's set up surveillance and monitor her. If we can track her movements and get better insight as to what she's doing, we'll have a better idea."

"You heard the man," Jason said to the voice on the phone before hanging up.

"That was some smart thinking, Drew."

"Thanks. I want to avoid killing an innocent person."

"Most hunters would have killed her, and if they were wrong, they'd rack her death up to collateral damage. After all, she does fit the bill of a newly turned werewolf."

"I know, but something just doesn't feel right."

"We'll take the time to observe her. However, there's only a few days before the full moon. If she's not the werewolf, we'll have lost several critical days of investigation. We need to look at the town from a different angle."

"What do you have in mind?"

"I'm thinking a cocky teenager who blares his music too loud and goes out of his way to offend everyone he meets just might piss off the right person. If the werewolf gets mad, it might go after the teenager."

Drew's stomach turned. "You mean me, don't you?"

"All you have to do is drive into town in one of the jeeps. Act as rude as you can, and draw enough attention to yourself to irritate the werewolf. Maybe drive over a lawn or two. Remember, the werewolf loves this town. Watching you disrespect it could set it off. Once you've pissed off enough people, drive a few miles out of town. The tactical unit will be waiting."

"It's not a bad idea, but I'm not sure it'll work. Besides, what happens if it attacks before I can get to the unit?"

"You'll be fine. Just make sure you have a shotgun and your knife with you."

Jason could tell Drew wasn't comfortable with the plan, but he ignored Drew's fears.

"Let's get you changed and get a jeep ready," Jason said as he took Drew's shoulder and nudged him forward out of the command tent.

# 3
# DREW THE PUNK

In just over an hour, Drew was behind the wheel of a jeep with the top off and the radio blasting Alice Cooper. The music was loud enough that he wore earplugs to prevent damage to his hearing. Just before he pulled into town, he double-checked to make sure his sawed-off shotgun was still under the seat and his silver knife was secure under his jean jacket.

Drew drove into town as fast as he could, being careful to sit just on the edge of the legal limit. Getting a ticket would be no big deal, but if he was arrested it would screw up the entire plan. He drove through town, cutting cars off and making fast hard turns, squealing the tires whenever possible. Once he felt he had drawn enough negative attention from the town folk who had to scurry out of his way, he slammed on his brakes and parked the jeep on the sidewalk in front of Franky's.

Drew walked in and plopped himself down in a booth near the windows.

"Hey!" he shouted across the crowded restaurant. "What do I have to do to get a damn cheeseburger in this dump?"

He was very uncomfortable with his charade. He felt sorry for the old couple sitting behind him, especially when they got up and left to avoid him.

A young woman, her long brown hair pulled back in a ponytail, came over to his table.

"What can I get you?" she asked reluctantly.

"Hey, babe. Get me a cheeseburger, fries and a Coke. And hurry the hell up, will you? I don't want to spend a minute longer in this dump than I have to."

"The feeling is mutual," the woman mumbled under her breath as she shuffled away.

Drew continued to be difficult, banging his fork and knife on the table and singing "School's Out for Summer" at the top of his lungs. The other customers were growing more and more annoyed. The waitress returned a few minutes later and dropped his plate in front of him.

He took one bite of the burger and spit it on the floor.

"What kind of crap is this?" he shouted.

A balding middle-aged man stormed out from the kitchen.

"What's your problem, kid?"

"This burger is crap. Is this what passes for food in this dive?"

"If you don't like it, feel free to leave."

"What if I don't want to leave?" Drew stood up.

"Betty! Call the sheriff!" the man yelled over his shoulder.

"What the hell? You make a crappy burger and now you call the sheriff?"

"That's right, kid."

"Screw you, man, and this waste of a town."

Drew pushed his way past the man, rushed out the front door and hopped in the jeep. As he pulled away from the restaurant, he almost hit a young man walking on the sidewalk.

"Get out of my way! I'm trying to drive here!" he screamed at the shocked young man.

The tires squealed as the jeep bounced off the sidewalk and hit the road. Drew pointed the vehicle in the direction of the town border and slammed down on the accelerator.

Once he was out of sight, Drew turned down the music and pulled out a radio from the glove box.

"Punk One to Overseer. Come in, Overseer. Over," he said into the radio.

"Go ahead, Punk. Over," Jason replied.

"I didn't like it, but I did the best I could. Over."

"Good work. Stay alert. The tactical unit is just up the road. Over."

"Copy that. Out."

Drew put the radio in his pocket and turned the music back up. He wasn't enjoying the volume of the music, but he wanted to make sure the werewolf could hear him from as far away as possible.

A few miles outside of town, Drew spotted a red flag sticking out of the top of an orange traffic cone sitting on the side of the road. The surveillance units used the cone to distract and slow down traffic. This allowed the team time to write down the license plates of any passing cars. Seeing the cone, Drew knew his team was close.

The beast burst out of the trees too fast for Drew to react. It smashed into the passenger side of the jeep, sending it flying off the road. The vehicle rolled repeatedly. The only thing that saved him was the seat belt, holding him tightly against his seat, and the jeep's roll bar, which kept it from being crushed. As the vehicle rolled, the shotgun became dislodged from its hiding place. Drew was able to grab the gun just as it was about to fly out. Once he settled in a ditch, he looked at the road and saw the massive werewolf barreling down on him.

He raised the shotgun and fired. The werewolf hurtled away from the jeep and out of sight. Even though Drew was upside down and disoriented, he was sure he'd hit the monster.

He unhooked the seatbelt and rolled out of his seat. Jumping to his feet, he scanned the area. The werewolf was close and hiding somewhere in the trees.

Crashing sounds echoed through the woods behind him. Drew swung the shotgun around and fired without aiming. The werewolf dodged the silver pellets and pounced closer to its prey. Drew pumped and fired again and again, each time missing his target. The beast leaped closer with each missed shot.

The animal jumped from a large tree stump and extended its claws toward Drew's throat. Its massive form blocked out the sky. As he racked the last round into the shotgun and fired a moment before the werewolf landed on him, Drew knew that even if the shot hit its mark, he was dead. There was no way he was going to avoid being impaled by the monster's claws.

# 4
# WHY DO YOU CARE?

The tactical unit raced down the road toward the sounds of the gunfire. Two jeeps and a truck stopped where Drew's wrecked jeep had come to rest. Ten armed men poured out and covered the area.

"I found him," one of the men yelled, getting Jason's attention.

Jason ran over to find Drew lying under a middle-aged man. Blood soaked the ground.

"Drew! Drew, can you hear me? Are you all right?" he yelled as he examined his partner for signs of life.

"I'm fine," Drew said from under the man. "Get this thing off me."

Two men lifted the body.

"Are you hurt? Did it bite you?" Jason asked.

"I don't think so. I have a few new bruises, but I don't feel like I broke anything major."

"Can you walk?"

"Help me up, and we'll find out."

Jason helped Drew to his feet.

"You're one lucky kid. Not many hunters could kill a werewolf by themselves."

"Lucky is right. Lucky for me the jeep held out and the shotgun fell into my hands. I could've been killed." Drew was visibly shaken and upset.

As Drew was checked over and subsequently cleared by the team medic, Jason reminded him, "In this job, we come close to death all the time. Luck is all you can hope for sometimes. Let's get you back home; your father will want to debrief you."


A few hours later, they were back on the modified cargo plane and headed home to Missouri.

Dan greeted the plane as it landed and hugged his son as soon as Drew's feet touched the ground.

"I heard what happened. I'm so glad you're okay."

"I'm fine, Dad. Not even a concussion."

"That's good to hear. Now we celebrate my son's first kill!" Dan shouted, firing up the other hunters. "Let the others unload the plane. You and I need to talk before the feast."

"Do we really need to have the feast?" Drew asked.

"We always feast a hunter's first lone kill. You should be proud and allow your fellow hunters to celebrate with you. Come on, your mother will want to hear all about your mission." Dan put an arm around his son, and led him to a waiting pickup truck. He drove from the small airport and up a dirt road. "Did you really leave that waitress a business card?"

Drew laughed. "I gave her the number of a counselor in the next town."

"Really? Why'd you do that?"

"She's depressed and could use someone to talk to, and I thought she'd prefer someone from out of town. I looked up counselors in the phone book and left the number of one on her front door."

"What made you think she's depressed?"

"As part of my tactical training, I studied a few books on psychology. I was hoping to understand how people react to situations. The indicators of a newly turned werewolf match that of a depressed person: they can become withdrawn and stop caring about their physical appearance."

"Once the waitress was cleared, she was no longer your problem. Why do you care?"

Drew looked over at his father with complete seriousness. He'd felt he should do something to help the woman they'd almost killed; it didn't feel right to have pried so deeply into her personal life, all for nothing. "We see so much death in our job. If I stopped caring about people, all I have left is killing."

"I never thought of it that way. So tell me about the werewolf."

"He was a local deputy and a hiker. From what we've been able to find out, he went on a hike near the Mexico border about six months ago, and I can only speculate that he was bitten during that trip. We found the bodies of his victims buried under his house. Luckily he killed them; otherwise we would be looking at an infestation of werewolves."

"What about cleanup?"

"We dropped a story about a horrid smell coming from his house. The police found the bodies of the missing people. As for him, we left him in his car and torched it in a ditch. No one will ever suspect he didn't die in a car accident, and he will never harm anyone again. We're also buying into the mine to ensure no one is suspicious of our cover story. It should bring in a nice return on the investment."

"Do you have any idea why he started to hunt humans? A werewolf doesn't normally go on killing sprees without a reason."

"He's a lone wolf with no pack to help guide or protect him. A new werewolf would suffer from aggression and severe impulse control issues. I doubt he could control himself without the support of a pack. Most likely, he probably lost his temper and bit someone. Once a werewolf tastes human blood, they crave human blood. It's probably a blessing he killed his victims, or we could be dealing with a pack of blood-crazed werewolves. No idea. He didn't keep a diary or leave clues behind. Probably got pissed off at someone and didn't know enough not to bite them."

"Good work, son."

The truck pulled up to a group of cabins hidden in the woods. Before Drew could get out, people started to gather and clap for him, patting him on the back and congratulating him on his successful mission. He thanked as many as he could as he made his way through the crowd.

His mother ran toward him and gave him a big hug and kiss.

"My boy is all grown up," she said, tears trickling down her cheek. She hugged him tight enough that he was having trouble breathing.

"Let the boy breathe," Dan said, pulling his wife off their son. "He needs to get cleaned up before the feast. You can fuss on him then."

Dan led his son away from the group, and into their family's cabin.

"What was that all about?" Drew asked.

"You're a hero now. You'd better get used to the attention."

"I didn't ask to be a hero."

"None of us ever do, but it's in our blood. Hunters know the dangers of our chosen profession. They've seen the evil in this world, and they've heard the story of Dracula. Today, you have proven yourself to be a true descendant of the great Abraham Van Helsing and a real hero. Besides, being a hero isn't such a bad thing. Heroes bring people hope, and considering what we hunt, hope can be in short supply at times."

Drew finished changing into clean clothes after washing his face. "What if I let them down?" he asked as he tucked in his shirt.

"You won't. By the way, considering how well you did on your mission, I want you to considering taking a position with the intelligence unit."

"Really? I like tactics, and it feels like a good fit."

"You do have a gift for planning, but we could really use your skills on the intelligence squad. From what I hear, you're a quick thinker and a great actor. We need men like you to be the tip of the spear. The intelligence squad goes in first and may find itself without backup at times. It's not an easy job, so I only ask the best of the hunters to join."

"All right, Pop, I'll give it a shot."

"Great. Now let's get to the party before your mother hunts me."

# 5
## WHICH WITCH

Drew quickly adapted to his new position. He was careful and never made assumptions, preferring instead to take his time and find the right target before ever letting an innocent person die, even if it meant the creature escaped.

Although he was always professional, he quickly got a reputation for putting his own life on the line to draw out the monster they were hunting. He took risks, but he always had a plan. Jason swore he was in more danger of Drew giving him a heart attack than a monster attack.

Within a couple short years on the job, Drew's acting became nearly flawless. With his age and looks, he could act as an older teenager or a young man. Once, he even played the role of a real estate investor so he could gain access to a house used as a vampire nest. Shortly after his twentieth birthday, Drew took on his best role yet.

The team hadn't even settled in from their last mission when Jason called everyone to the briefing room. Drew was still cleaning his gun when the call came down to gear up.

"Have any of you ever been to an amusement park?" Jason asked as he entered the briefing room.

A couple of the team members raised their hands. "Good. The rest of you will soon get your chance." He handed out pictures of a park called Six Flags Over Texas.

Drew was amazed at all the rides and shows. The place looked incredible. He was curious about the mission, but he was more concerned about getting a chance to ride the new Runaway Mine Train roller coaster.

"Local police have been getting reports of kids getting unexplainably sick during or just after visiting the park. It opened a few years ago just outside Dallas. Until now, there have only been a few injuries and a lot of upset stomachs from too much junk food."

A few people laughed at Jason's joke.

"Recently kids, ages one to seventeen, have been getting extremely tired and many are passing out. Three kids have even died. Doctors can't link this sickness to anything in the park or find any logical explanation. The Center for Disease Control was contacted, but so far they haven't been any help."

"Are we looking for a witch?" Scott Grimes, a tactical unit sniper, asked from the back of the room.

"We aren't sure. For all of you who don't remember your Monsters of the World lessons, witches come in two forms, but both feed off children. A good witch won't harm you or attack an innocent. They use their magic to heal and protect. Good witches surround themselves with children and gain strength from their happiness. They are normally very beautiful and enticing."

A few offhand jokes circled the room about Jason being a witch lover. He ignored them.

"A bad or dark witch uses children for food. Their lust for flesh makes them very ugly and very powerful. They are harder to kill than vampires and just as deadly. Once discovered, a witch will normally retreat, but don't think they won't kill you if you try to stop them."

"How do we fight them?" This question came from Roberto Clausin, the team medic.

"Normal weapons will slow them down. The more powerful and evil they are, the more of an effect silver will have on them. To kill one, you have to take off her head or burn the body past the point of rejuvenation. Some believe magic will hurt them, but unless any of you are wizards, I don't think that applies."

Jason received a few more snickers with his last joke.

"What's the plan?" Drew asked.

Jason looked at him. "You tell me. How would you lure a witch?"

Drew took a few seconds to review the pictures. "If we're looking for a witch, she'll be near an area with lots of kids. She would want access to the park as often as possible. It might be an employee of the park or she might be nesting somewhere close. Shutting down the park to make her move would raise too much suspicion. We should go in as employees and look for anyone getting too close to the kids."

"It can't be a witch," said Glenda Rex, Drew's partner from the intelligence unit.

"Why?" Jason asked.

"If it's a good witch, the kids wouldn't be getting sick. A good witch would die before she hurt a child. A bad witch would be taking the children and cooking them, but not nearly at the rate these kids are getting sick," she replied.

"You might be right. We may be dealing with some sort of demon—or even just a new type of food poisoning. That's why I want you guys to get new jobs."

Drew glanced at Glenda. Glenda was at least ten years older than Drew, but she seemed just as excited as he was to be getting a job at an amusement park. Drew couldn't wait to ride all the rides and taste all the different food. The team would set up a place nearby for him to live, but most of his free time could be spent at the park.

Drew knew he was going to have the time of his life and if things worked out, he would get to hunt a witch. There was nothing more he could have asked for in an assignment.

# 6
# PLEASE KILL ME

Working at the amusement park wasn't exactly what Drew had imagined. He took a job as a janitor working the evening shift. This allowed him to walk the park during the day and his work kept him there well after the park closed for the night. As the new guy at the park, he got the most disgusting assignments, but when he wasn't cleaning up some kid's puke, he was able to walk the entire park with a broom and dust pan. No one ever paid much attention to the janitors, so no one ever noticed the small bulge of his pistol tucked under his blue-gray jumpsuit.

Glenda had a hard time concealing her weapon at first. She took a job as a secretary in the main office and had to resort to carrying a big purse to keep her gun hidden. By the third day, she was already complaining that her job didn't make her feel useful on the mission and she hated having to wear a skirt to work every day.

By the end of the first week, Drew had a possible suspect. The first day on the job, he had noticed an elderly woman sitting on a bench. Since a witch could reverse the aging process, he'd ruled her out at first, assuming she was probably someone's grandmother. After seeing her multiple days in a row, he knew something wasn't right.

For as many times as he saw her, the woman never spoke to a single person. Each day she would show up on a different bench in the park and wouldn't move until the park was about to close. Since she didn't seem to be actively trying to harm children, Drew decided to wait to approach her until he could devise a plan.

Two days later, he went to the park as was normal. Instead of riding rides and trying different foods from around the world, he searched the park for the woman. He found her in less than an hour, sitting near the

Enemy Fort exhibit.

Drew stepped away from the crowds and gave his position to the team over the radio. Unlike other days, this time the tactical unit was walking through the park in plain clothes. If the witch tried to attack, she would face ten armed professionals ready to take her down. Against Jason's recommendation, Drew wanted to talk to her first, just to be sure she was the witch. It was risky but he had to be sure.

Once he knew the tactical unit was ready to strike, Drew walked up to the bench and took a seat next to the old woman.

"Have you come to kill me?" the woman asked before he could say a word.

"Do you know me?" He couldn't help showing his surprise at her question.

"No, but I know your bloodline. I can smell it on you. Your ancestor was the Helsinger boy, was he not?"

Drew knew his family's history traced back to the first human hunter. A boy named Von Helsinger had started a war on magic and freed humanity from slavery. The family had taken the Van Helsing name in his honor.

"That is what I've been told," he replied.

"I assume you still fight for his cause to destroy all magic. I won't fight you. Do what you must."

He was stunned by her willingness to die so quickly.

"You don't seem evil. Why are you hurting the children?"

"I don't mean to. I came here to be amongst them. The children here are so happy; I just want to embrace their joy. It's their fear that I didn't consider."

"What do you mean?"

"When a child is afraid, I naturally try to pull their fear from them. A scared child is a horrible thing to feel. In this place, a child's fear is replaced with happiness very quickly. At times, the switch has been too fast for me to react, and as a result, I end up pulling at their happiness. This is why they're getting sick."

"Why don't you leave?"

"I wish I could, but all the fear has made me weak. I'm too weak to leave the park; I'm even too weak to fight off aging. The weaker I get, the harder it is for me to control myself. I try to focus on just the happiness in the hopes of rebuilding my strength, but the fear keeps pulling at me."

"You don't leave the park? Where do you go?"

"I've been hiding in the woods. Please, just kill me and stop me from hurting any more children."

Drew sat back on the bench and considered his options.

"If you were able to leave, what would happen to you?"

"If I could find a place with happy children, away from the fear, I would regain my strength and never come back to a place like this."

"What if I were able to help you? Do you trust me enough to come with me?"

"I don't need to trust you. I'm ready to die for what I've done. The deaths of those children are on my head, and I can never forgive myself."

"I don't think killing you is necessary, but you can't stay here. Come with me, and I'll do what I can to help you make amends."

"I always knew your bloodline was special, but I never would've imagined you helping me."

"What's your name?" he asked as he took her arm and helped her off the bench.

The woman looked back at him with confusion. "You know, I've been alone for so many years, I don't even remember," she admitted. "I'm sure it'll come back to me."

"For now, how about we call you Harriet, after Harriet Stowe."

"Who's Harriet Stowe?"

"I read about her in the Enemy Fort exhibit right over there." He pointed to the exhibit nearby. "It just seems like a good name to pick for you."

"Was she a witch?"

"Not that I know of. She wrote a book about slavery and did a lot to help keep runaway slaves safe, even though she was breaking the law. Her story kind of reminds me of your situation. You come to the park every day to help children even though it's hurting you. It just seems fitting that you use her name for now."

"I like that name," she replied as they walked together.

Jason wasn't happy with Drew's decision but he respected him enough to go along with his plan. Within a few hours the team had packed up their gear and was on the plane headed for home.

"What were you thinking, bringing that witch here?" Dan asked Drew after the plane landed.

"She's not evil. She was trapped at the park by fear. I had two choices: kill her or help her escape the situation. I thought she could help us. She can help watch the children, heal the wounded and even help protect us with magic."

"For centuries, our family has hunted anything magical."

"If she causes even the slightest problem, I will kill her myself."

Dan looked at his son with frustration but was quick to recognize he had done the right thing. "You still amaze me, son. You really are a hero."

The two men hugged and went back to the plane to help unload the equipment.

Jason and two of his men were standing guard over Harriet.

"Miss Harriet," Dan said as they returned, "my son has convinced me to allow you to live amongst us. You'll remain under guard and must promise not to cast any spells until we know you can be trusted. If you step out of line—or we even suspect you of casting spells—we will kill you."

"I understand," she said. "The Helsinger men are not known for compassion. I thank you for helping me."

"Singer is the name now. I am Dan Singer, leader of the finest group of hunters known to man."

"You know, you kind of remind me of Von," she said, giving him an inquisitive look.

"You mean Von Helsinger, the man who started the war against magic?"

"The last time I saw him he was a boy, but you and your son both have his eyes and his heart."

"When you get settled, you'll have to tell us the story of Von. Around here he is a legend."

"I'll tell you everything I can remember."

"First let's go and meet the children. We have several families in camp, and it would be nice to have another pair of eyes to watch over them."

# 7

# THE TEACHER

Harriet fit in perfectly. The children loved her caring heart, and she enjoyed watching and teaching them. Jason and his men watched her closely at first, but she didn't mind their company.

After a couple of days, she requested a meeting with Dan.

Drew tagged along. If something went wrong, it was his job to protect his father. He suspected she just wanted to talk, but tensions were still very high amongst the hunters concerning her presence, and Drew hoped his own presence at the meeting would quash any fears…and hopefully the men would feel better about their leader being near her.

"You asked to speak to me?" Dan walked up to Harriet, who was busy helping a group of children make Mother's Day cards out of construction paper.

"Dan, how good of you to come."

Harriet seemed much happier in her new surroundings. Her voice no longer sounded as if she were struggling for breath; instead it sounded as if she were singing every word with the harmony of a bird.

"I'm glad to see you brought your son. I was hoping to talk to you both."

"It's good to see you happy," Drew said. He was surprised she still looked like an old woman. "You seem much stronger than before; why haven't you changed your appearance?"

"I have you to thank for my strength. Without your help, I would've died a horrible death. I haven't changed because I agreed to follow the rules. Reversing the aging process takes magic and I swore not to use any."

"Don't you want to be young again?"

"I have everything I could have ever asked for. The children are happy and I no longer feel the poison of fear. When they're afraid, I've found that telling stories to them about you seems to calm them. You are a true hero to these people."

"Why did you wish to speak to me?" Dan asked.

"I promised you a chance to hear about Von and what happened so long ago. I want to keep my promise. Now that I'm stronger, most of my memory has returned and I'm ready to tell you anything you wish to hear."

"That's great news. Why don't we spread the word so the others can join us? We'd all love to hear a good story."

"That sounds lovely."

Word spread fast, and soon every able body gathered around the picnic tables, ready to hear what Harriet had to say about the first hunter. She sat on the bench and turned so she was facing a group of children sitting on the ground in front of her.

"I can't remember how my life started, but I know I was traveling with a very powerful wizard named Oni. Oni was my friend and my teacher. We traveled to a city that didn't like wizards, but Oni was on a mission. We decided to hide our abilities so we could avoid trouble with the soldiers.

"During our time in the city I met Von, but he was not the great warrior you know. Back then, he was just a boy, no older then twelve. A large storm had separated him from his family and all he wanted was to find a way home. Oni and I felt sorry for him and wanted to help him."

"When the Dragon King set a trap for Von, he came to Oni and me and begged us to go with him. Oni knew the darkest and meanest of all wizards was going to attack the city, so he asked me to stay and protect the people of the city. I did my best, but the evil wizard's army was just too strong. I barely escaped with my life."

"As time passed, I heard stories of an army of humans defying all magic. The army was strong and quickly became feared by all magical creatures, even the Dragon King. The leader of the army was rumored to be immortal, and even the fire of a dragon could not hurt him. The leader was none other than young Von Helsinger. It was rumored that he had even faced the four elementals and made them back down from his blade."

"Von led the humans across the land of magic, killing anyone who wanted to hurt or enslave them. After years of war, the Dragon King called for an end to the war, but the only way Von would give up the fight was if the Dragon King and the wizards were no longer on the earth."

"The Dragon King was helpless against Von and his army; he had no choice but to give Von want he wanted. He called a meeting with the most powerful wizards and demanded that magic return to the earth where it came from. No one knows what happened to the Dragon King or the wizards, but magic changed that day. Wizards no longer controlled the elements as we once did. Some wizards lost their powers completely, while others adapted to the new ways of magic."

"I became weak and almost died. Magic took pity on me and allowed me to learn the new ways. I had become what you know as a good witch. I found a position in the human army as a healer and stayed strong by bringing joy to those around me."

"After the war was over, Von continued his fight by hunting down those who still possessed the ability to use magic. He fought his entire life, knowing nothing but war. Even though he saw enough death for a thousand life times, Von's heart never blackened. He remained dedicated to protecting humans and always gave of himself to save others."

"What happened to him?" one of the children asked.

"No one knows. I know Von married a young woman and built a small house to raise his children. There are many rumors about how he died. Some say a demon attacked and killed him and his family, others say Von died an old man, watching his children have children of their own. The most popular rumor at the time was that Gaia herself took Von from the world so she could enjoy it once again."

"What do you believe?" Drew asked.

"I believe that no matter what happened to his body, his spirit has lived on in you fine hunters. Now it is your turn to fight and protect the humans. I know Von would be proud of all of you, no matter where he is now."

The group asked a few more questions before Harriet called it quits.

"It's late; we should get some dinner and maybe we can have a campfire afterward. What do you say?" she asked the children, who all cheered at the idea.

Dan and Drew thanked her for sharing Von's story, and then Dan said something that completely surprised Drew.

"If you want to make yourself younger, go ahead. You can also help out with the sick and injured if you're up to it."

"Thank you, Dan. Rejuvenating myself is one thing, but aren't you worried that seeing me use magic on a regular basis, even as a healer, will upset the others?"

"You might be right. Stick to being with the children for now. I'll let the doctor know you're available to help with anything too big for him."

Harriet lowered her hands to her waist and slowly brushed them up her torso and over her face and hair. As her hands moved, her muscles became stronger and she started to stand up straighter. Her face and skin tightened. Her wiry grey hair grew soft and turned to a beautiful shade of mocha brown.

"How do I look?" she asked.

"Beautiful," Jason stammered, standing nearby.

Drew didn't say it aloud, but he agreed.

# 8
# RESTLESS SPIRITS

Before the year was up, Jason had proposed to Harriet, and they were now planning a spring wedding. Harriet had proven herself a critical part of the team. She still spent most of her time with the children, but she also took care of things like the flu bug and common colds that normally took days to get over.

During his free time, Drew would talk to her about the different creatures she knew. He wanted to know how they acted and what motivated them. His line of questioning always piqued her curiosity.

"When most hunters ask about the different magical creatures in the world, all they want to know is how to kill them. Why do you care about their way of life?" Harriet asked Drew after discussing imps.

"I believe you have to know your enemy in order to defeat them," he answered. "Destroying an army only leads to the defeat of the ruler, but if you know what motivates your enemy you can defeat their way of life."

"I find it hard to believe you want to know how to destroy a creature's way of life."

"I don't, really, but understanding them will help me defeat them. Take a vampire, for example. Vampires feed to survive. They become controlled by their hunger and they don't care who they kill. If we can find a pattern in their feeding habits, we may be able to set up a trap. Then we can keep the fight away from people and reduce collateral damage."

"A vampire won't die easily."

"I know, but by understanding their weakness, even the strongest vampire can be killed."

"Isn't it enough to shoot them full of silver?"

"That will kill them, but how do you get close enough to get a shot? If we didn't understand the weaknesses of vampires, we wouldn't know about their aversion to garlic or holy water."

"You're a very smart young man and a fine hunter."

"There is one thing I don't understand."

"It would be my honor to help you any way I can."

"Why do you never talk about demons? Did they not exist during the time of magic?"

"That's not an easy question for me to answer. I don't know much about the spirit world. What I do know may only confuse you more."

"Try me."

"Humanity is divided when it comes to their religious beliefs. Some believe in a single God; others believe there are several different gods, each with their own powers. Some believe in a heaven and hell; other religions believe in reincarnation. This division is not about right or wrong as many believe; it's simply a matter of how people explain what they don't understand."

"Do you know which religion is right?"

"In a way, they all are. You asked about demons. Some religions see demons as a sort of evil—or agents of hell. As far as I can tell, demons are nothing more than spirits, trapped and unable to move on to whatever is waiting for them…if anything is waiting for them, that is."

"What makes them attack humans?"

"It could be anything. Most of them just want to find answers, but there are some that want to destroy humanity. I think those demons are tied to magic somehow and they are trying to make humans pay for what Von started."

"If they're motivated by trying to move on, but there's nothing to go to, how can they be appeased?"

"Like I said, I don't know much about the spirit world, but when the Dragon King insisted that magic return to the earth, it changed. It adapted in order to survive. This is when magical items and places started to appear."

"Are you saying magic is a spirit?"

"In a way, I suppose. Gaia gives life, not gifts. Magic is not a living being like humans, but it does have a life."

"Huh…" Drew started to stare off into space as if he were devising a plan.

"What are you thinking?"

"I'm just wondering if there's a way to defeat magic. If magic is a living being, than it must be driven by some motivation."

"Most likely, that motivation is to survive."

"Which would explain why it didn't return to the earth as planned. Maybe if I understood magic better, I could find a way to use it or even defeat it."

"I don't understand."

"Before World War II, the Japanese people viewed their emperor as a god. After the war, the Japanese no long saw the emperor in such a way, and it changed their entire culture. Defeating the army wasn't enough, but by defeating their god, the entire country changed."

"So if you could find a way to defeat magic, you think all that follow it will change?"

"Maybe. But how do you defeat a spirit?"

"Now you sound like a hunter."

"I am a hunter, but maybe magic doesn't need to be my enemy."

"I almost feel sorry for whoever is your enemy," she said with a smile.

# 9

# FRIENDS AT GUNPOINT

By the time Drew turned twenty-four, Dan had given him his own team to lead. With three complete teams, the hunters were able to focus on training and still handle the different missions that came to their attention. Dan and Jason led their teams by coordinating with both the tactical and intelligence units, but Drew still preferred to go in and gather intelligence himself. Since he was not always in contact with the tactical unit, Drew required his team to think on their feet and be ready for anything. This also meant he had to lay out a solid plan before he ever started his mission.

After a long week of training to track werewolves in an urban environment, Drew called a meeting with his team. Since the other two teams weren't on a hunt, Dan and Jason decided to sit in on the meeting.

"First, I want to say that you all did very well with training this week. I know hunting a werewolf in a town is difficult, but you handled it very well. I think all week we only let the target escape one time," Drew said as the team gathered. The team clapped, satisfied with their success.

Once the applause calmed down, Drew continued with what he had to say.

"We have a mission, and this one is close to home. In the last month, several farmers have reported increased wolf attacks on livestock outside St. Louis. The farmers are pointing the blame at the newly built Endangered Wolf Center opened by Dr. Marlin Perkins and his wife, Carol. Normally, wolf attacks would be handled by the local government, but there have been no tracks found near any of the attacks."

"That doesn't make any sense. What's attacking the livestock? Even werewolves leave tracks," Glenda asked from the audience.

"I don't know. It could be a vampire with a taste for livestock, or some sort of demon. We're going to have to spread out on this one. The tactical unit will be split, and we'll go and talk to the farmers as investigators for the Wild Life Commission. Glenda is going to take a job at the Wolf Center as a volunteer."

"All work and no pay," she said jokingly. The team laughed.

"I think my dad will still sign your pay check." The group laughed again. "I'm going to be visiting the different towns in the area as a graduate student. I'll be looking for anything that points to an angry spirit. Look for patterns or anything that might indicate a motive besides feeding. Since we don't know what we're facing, everyone should load up with silver and bring a silver knife."

He spent the next twenty minutes going over details of the attacks and the plan. Once the group was dismissed, Drew walked over to Jason and his dad.

"Are you sure you don't want help with the investigation, son?"

"I think we can handle it. I don't want to flood the area with too many people; we might scare off whatever is behind these attacks. I would like to bring Harriet in on this one, though."

"Why do you want her?" Jason asked. "She's never been in the field, and now is definitely not the right time for her to be away."

Harriet had just given birth to their daughter, Amanda, less than a month before. Jason was such a proud dad; he'd showed everyone in camp her picture at least twice already.

"I'm not asking her to go into the field, but she knows a lot about different creatures. I was hoping to have her go over the reports and anything we might find. She might be able to find some similarities to a creature we haven't considered."

"I think it's a great idea," Dan added. "As long as she's up to it."

Jason was happy his wife was being included, but was worried the work would cause her too much stress.

"I'll ask her, as long as she doesn't have to do any fighting."

"You do realize you married a witch," Drew said mockingly. "She's older than anything we've ever faced and stronger than all of us."

"She's still my wife. Maybe one day you'll understand what that means."

"I promise I would never put her in harm's way."

"I'll ask her, but you'd better come back in one piece."

"I have a feeling that most of the time, I'll have my nose buried in dusty old history books."

The next day, the team set off for the two-hour drive toward St Louis. Drew drove by himself in a run-down old jeep. He carried a backpack and several books on history and hauntings to look the part. His pistol was safely tucked under his jacket along with his knife. He also stored a sawed-off shotgun under the seat, just in case.

For the next week, Drew drove from town to town, searching historical archives and death certificates. He was looking for anything that might talk about a haunting or a horrible death. There were several possibilities, but nothing that included animals.

Every chance he could, he called back to the main camp to get status updates from the rest of the team. No one had found anything useful.

On the seventh day, Drew pulled into the small town of New Haven, Missouri. He talked to a few locals and they told him a story of an old bridge that was haunted by a pack of dogs. It was his first possible lead. It wasn't much to work with, but it was a start.

That night, he made his way to the haunted bridge and pulled off to the side of the road. He heard the sounds of dogs off in the distance as soon as he reached the center of the bridge. Drew noted the direction of the sounds and made his way back to the jeep.

"Hold it right there, mister."

The female voice came from under the cover of a tree. A flashlight lit up the night, forcing him to cover his eyes. "What are you doing lurking around in the dark?" she asked.

He couldn't see who was talking, but decided to keep to his cover story.

"I'm a student researching Missouri's haunted places. This bridge has a lot of history," he replied.

"Then why did I find a shotgun in your jeep?" A female state trooper stepped out from the tree line. "Put your hands in the air and don't make any sudden moves."

Drew slowly put his hands up. "I use the shotgun for protection. My research takes me to some very rural places. I never know when I'm going to run into a wild animal."

"Do you think I'm an idiot? Don't lie to me. You have a professionally modified pump action Browning with custom rounds. I bet when I search you, I'll find a hand gun and maybe even a hunting knife. You're a poacher and you're under arrest. Now turn around and get on your knees."

Drew did as she commanded.

"I know you're only doing your job, and you have no reason to believe me, but I'm not a poacher. I don't hunt animals."

"Really? What do you hunt?" The officer grabbed his right wrist from behind and slapped a handcuff on him. She pulled his right arm down behind his back and grabbed his left wrist.

Drew rolled forward, sending the trooper over his head. He rose to his feet and aimed his pistol.

"Don't move. I don't want to hurt you. Roll on your stomach with your hands flat on the ground above your head," he commanded.

The officer complied.

"You're making a big mistake. You'll never get away with murdering a state trooper," she shouted.

"I told you, I'm not going to hurt you." He reached down and removed her revolver. He patted her down, and found a backup weapon strapped to her ankle. He quickly searched her pants pockets and found the keys to the handcuffs.

"Sorry about the invasion of privacy, but I can't let you take me to jail. At least not until my assignment is completed."

"What assignment? What are you, some sort of spy?"

Drew put her guns in his jeep.

"You can sit up if you would be more comfortable," he told her.

The officer rolled on to her back and sat up.

"I'll tell you what I'm doing, but you won't believe me. I'm a monster hunter, and I'm investigating the recent attacks on livestock in the area."

"You're a monster hunter? Do you think I'm stupid?"

"I get it. It's hard to believe, but let me ask you this: How else do you explain that there have been no tracks found from a wolf or any other animal at any of the attacks?"

"Are you serious?"

"Unfortunately I am. I think there's a demon in the area and it won't be long before it turns its attention to humans. I'm here to kill it."

"All right, monster hunter, what do you plan to do with me?"

"That's up to you. I can lock you in your trunk and leave you. I'll call the police in the morning and tell them where I left you. Then you'll probably put out an APB and start a statewide manhunt for me. The people against female troopers will use this incident as a reason to try to get rid of you, and my mission will be compromised. Neither one of us wants those things to happen."

"What's my second choice?"

"Help me find the demon and put an end to this before someone gets hurt. Afterward, you can join my team or go back to being a trooper."

"There are more of you?"

"Several, and we're all well trained in hunting. We have former police officers join us all the time. It's not a glamorous job, but at the end of the day, we know we're protecting people from their worst nightmares."

"If I agree to help you, how do you know I won't try to escape or arrest you?"

"With all the death and evil I see in the world, I know when I can trust a person. If you give me your word that you want to help and won't try anything, then I'll believe you. It's your call."

"You don't seem crazy, and I really don't want to be locked in a trunk all night. All right, hunter, I'll help."

"Welcome to the team." Drew reached out his hand to help the woman off the ground. "Drew Singer," he said, introducing himself as he took off the handcuffs.

"Pat Starboard."

"Nice to meet you, Pat. Now, can I have my shotgun back?"

# 10
# WARGS

Pat followed Drew into town where he made two phone calls. The first was to her commanding officer, explaining that the U.S. Department of Agriculture had recruited her to help in the investigation of the attacks. Drew promised to have a couple officers drop off the paperwork in the morning.

His second call was to his father.

"Dad, I think I found something. There's a bridge where you can hear dogs barking in the distance. I need to meet up with some of the team and try to triangulate the sound."

"Sounds like you've been busy," Dan replied. "Jason and Harriet are leaving soon and should reach you by tonight. They need to know where to meet you."

Drew knew better than to ask questions during an operation. It was part of the training that you trusted the judgment of the team no matter what.

"I'm in New Haven now, but I can get a hotel room in Wentzville for the night. We can meet at the hotel in the morning. Have them bring some silver rounds for a Smith & Wesson Model 60."

Dan understood the rules during an operation as well as Drew. "Anything else you need?"

"I need a couple members from the tactical unit, and paperwork saying that a Missouri State Trooper named Pat Starboard will be assigned to the U.S. Department of Agriculture during the investigation."

"They'll have it with them. Make sure you talk to them before you do anything, and stay safe."

"Will do, Dad," Drew replied, and hung up. "We have to meet some of the team in Wentzville tomorrow," he told Pat.

"What are we going to do until then?"

"I suggest we get a couple of hotel rooms and I can brief you on everything we know so far."

"I'll need a change of clothes."

"Wear what you have on and we'll get you something to wear in the morning. What do you want to do with your car? You're cleared with your command and don't need to report in, but it might look funny to have your patrol car parked in front of a hotel all night."

Pat agreed, and they dumped the cruiser at the local police station. During the hour's drive to the hotel, Drew captivated her with accounts of his hunting adventures. He enjoyed talking to her. It was a nice change of pace to talk to someone who wasn't a hunter.

At the hotel, they booked adjoining rooms. The two of them discussed and reviewed the mission, and he showed her a map of all the locations of the attacks. He explained why he thought it wasn't a werewolf or a vampire and he described what their normal attacks should look like.

"You really know your stuff," she said after fatigue started to set in. "I think I'm going to take a hot shower and get some sleep."

Drew gave her one of his shirts to wear for the night, and sent her off to stay in the adjoining room. After she left the room, he took a shower and washed his clothes in the sink. He was starting to enjoy the nomadic life. He hadn't been able to stay in one location for more than a few days since the investigation started, but he'd learned quickly how to travel light with only a couple days' worth of clean clothes and a bar of laundry soap.

As he left the bathroom, he was surprised to see Pat sitting on the edge of his bed wearing nothing but the plaid button-up he had given her.

"Are you all right?" he asked as he stepped back into the bathroom holding the towel tightly around his waist.

"Do you ever get afraid?" she asked.

"Right now I'm afraid I am going to offend you. Can you throw me a pair of pants from my bag?"

A few moments later, a pair of pants landed just outside the bathroom door.

"Of course I get afraid," he said as he reached out and picked up the pants. "We all do; it's what we do with our fear that sets us apart from the average person. You should know this as a trooper." Drew stepped out of the bathroom after he was properly dressed.

"I just can't get the idea of being ripped apart by a pack of demon dogs out of my head."

"You have to trust me, my family has been hunting monsters for a long time."

"Your entire family does this?"

"We're kind of born into it."

"What does that mean?"

"Are you up to a history lesson?"

"I would listen to you tell me about your high school girlfriend if it took my mind off of demon dogs."

Drew took a seat in one of the two chairs by the window.

"Have you ever read Dracula?" he asked.

"No, but I saw the movie that came out a few years back." Pat sat down across from Drew.

"Did you ever wonder where the Van Helsing character learned how to kill Dracula?"

"Dracula was real?"

"Unfortunately, yes, he was. He terrorized Transylvania for centuries before he tried to move to England. Bram Stoker based his novel off a diary he found."

"So your last name is really Van Helsing?"

"It was changed shortly after my family came to America. The novel attracted a lot of unwanted attention to the hunters, and the Van Helsing name became death sentence."

"How did Van Helsing know how to kill a vampire?"

"My ancestors have been fighting monsters for 4000 years. There has been a lot of trial and error over the years."

"It amazes me that you know so much of your family history."

"In this line of work, it's foolish to ignore the past. Our enemies have a tendency to be a lot older and stronger than we are, so we have to be smarter."

"So have you faced demon dogs before?"

"We normally deal with more solid forms of the undead."

"I was wrong." Pat started to shake as her fears returned. "This conversation is not helping my fears at all."

"Take the shotgun. It might help you sleep."

"How about I take the bed?" Pat gave him a bit of a smile.

Drew was a little uncomfortable at what he thought she was implying. He was used to bunking with women during missions, but it was always business. For the first time, he noticed how beautiful Pat was, with her shoulder-length brown hair and very fit and slender body.

"Sure," he said nervously. "I'll camp out on the floor."

She smiled and the two of them settled in for the night.

Drew grabbed the pillows and comforter from the other room and lay down on the floor by the foot of the bed. He closed his eyes and tried to sleep. He nearly jumped out of his skin when he heard Pat speak.

"Drew?" Her voice seemed to echo in his head. "Are you still awake?"

"I am."

"I'm glad I didn't shoot you."

Drew chuckled. "So am I."

Drew woke up the next morning and gathered up his gear before waking Pat. "The team will be here shortly," he said. "After we meet up with them, we'll find a place to buy you some clothes."

"What about weapons?" Pat asked as she got dressed in the bathroom.

"Since we don't know what we're going to face, I'm not sure what we need. I have some silver rounds coming for you, and the shotgun is loaded with silver buckshot. Once we find the target, the tactical unit will do most of the heavy work. My job is to identify the target and get clear before the bullets start flying."

There was a knock on the door.

"Who is it?" Drew asked.

"It's the bullet and breakfast delivery service," Jason answered.

Drew flung open the door.

"You'd better not be kidding about the food," he said.

Jason held up a grocery bag.

"We got enough for all four of us. Who's the new guy, anyway?" Jason saw Pat standing in the room as he pushed his way in. "Or new girl."

"Jason Riley, meet Pat Starboard."

Pat stuck out her hand.

"Nice to meet you. Drew's told me a lot about you."

Harriet stepped into the room to see her husband frozen with surprise.

"It's nice to meet you too, dear," Harriet said like a caring grandmother. "Forgive my husband, but he is not used to seeing Drew step out of character on a mission. We guessed Drew had recruited some sort of master detective to help him."

Jason finally shook Pat's hand.

"Drew normally doesn't let his guard down, but then again, we don't normally work with beautiful cops," he said.

"She tried to arrest me," Drew said. "She had me dead to rights. I had to bring her in, or the mission would've been blown."

"We brought coffee and donuts for breakfast," Harriet said. "I hope you're hungry."

"Starved," Pat replied.

The four of them grabbed a donut or two and drank the tar that they called coffee from the nearby truck stop.

"I think I know what's attacking the livestock, or at least their motivation," Harriet said as she sat back and let her coffee cool.

"Before you say anything, I think Pat needs to know a bit more about you," Jason said interrupting his wife.

"I guess you're right. I'm sure you're a bit overwhelmed with all of this, but I'm going to make it a bit worse. I'm a witch. A good witch, mind you, but still a witch. I've been alive for thousands of years. When the earth was younger, there were all sorts of creatures not seen today. Drew asked me to think back in the hopes of finding some link to creatures from that time."

"You're right, you made it worse," Pat said, trying to absorb the new information.

"It'll be all right," Drew said, trying to calm Pat's nerves. "Harriet's on our side. She only wants to help."

"We don't have much time," Jason added. "I'm sorry, Pat, but we had to tell you this before someone else gets hurt."

"Someone else?" Drew asked.

"There was an attack last night near New Haven. A farmer was found dead in his field."

"That's horrible," Pat said.

"That's why we're here. We'll stop it. Drew's our best intelligence operator."

"Enough of the flattery," Drew interrupted. "Harriet, tell me what you're thinking."

"I remember orcs used to train their wargs to hunt by killing livestock. They'd train them to attack a specific target amongst a field. When a human would get out of line or escape, the orcs would release the wargs to kill them."

"You think we're after wargs?" Drew asked.

"What's a warg?" Pat added.

"A warg is a larger, wild, dog-like creature. Orcs would ride them into battle like horses. I doubt we're dealing with wargs, but it appears that someone is using the same training method. We don't know what caused them to attack a human."

"I think I know," Drew said. "I escaped from Pat yesterday evening on that bridge. I bet this hunter was looking for me."

"That does make sense," Jason said. "We were thinking the spirit of an old slaver was training ghost dogs to attack runaways. It must think you're a runaway."

"But why would it start now after all these years?" Pat asked.

"I don't believe spirits have a sense of time. They come back to the world whenever they get angry enough," Harriet answered.

"I know what we have to do. Can you two stick around for one night?" Drew asked.

"That depends on what you have in mind. Are you planning on giving me a heart attack?" Jason asked.

"Not if I can help it. Sorry, Pat. I need you to stay in your uniform a little longer."

# 11
# THE RUNNER

Pat pulled her patrol car on to the bridge. It seemed to get darker out as the time crept closer to midnight.

"Are you sure about this?" she asked Drew, who was sitting in the passenger seat.

"I have no idea if the spirit really attacked a human because I escaped. It could just be a coincidence. Right now, it's the only lead we have," Drew said as he checked his shotgun and strapped it to his back.

"What if you're right? It'll come after you. You could die."

"I'm going to be fine. My entire tactical unit is spread all over the path, and the farmhouse is only two miles away. Even running through the trees, I can make that in less than twenty minutes. If anything comes after me, it'll have to take on a solid form to attack. The snipers will have me covered. Once I get to the farmhouse, Jason and the others will help me make a stand."

"I'm worried about you," Pat said with a hint of sadness to her voice. She liked Drew and felt safe around him. Part of her thought he was completely insane and he was living in some sort of fantasy world, but she trusted him and didn't want to see him hurt.

"Don't worry; this is what I do. In a few hours, this will all be over." He looked down at his wrist watch. "It's time to get started."

The two of them stepped out of the car and Drew put a handcuff on his wrist.

"Do you want a head start?" she asked as she pulled her pistol.

"No. As soon as I take off, fire twice and call for the dogs. You ready?"

"Not if I can talk you out of this."

"You can't." Drew ran off down the bridge.

Two shots rang out. "He's escaping!" Pat yelled at the top of her lungs.

"Get the dogs!"

Drew immediately heard the dogs barking off in the distance. He ran as fast as he could over the rough terrain. As he passed by the first two guys from the tactical unit, he could feel a gun pointed in his direction. The barking dogs seemed to be getting closer. The plan had worked; now all he had to do was make it to the farmhouse.

Drew ran through the trees while staying as close as he could to the river that ran within yards of the farmhouse. If he got too far off track, no one would be able to help him. His entire ten-man tactical unit was in position near the river and they were his only backup if the dogs caught up to him quicker than planned.

The rocks and trees didn't make for an easy run. He had trained to run in full gear, but for some reason, running like this was really slowing him down. By the time he reached the end of his first mile, he was running about ten minutes per mile. He knew he had to speed up if he wanted any chance to make it.

The dogs sounded as if they were right on top of him. He knew better than to turn around. It would only slow him down.

A thick fog came from nowhere. It seemed to rise up from the ground itself. Within seconds, the fog crawled up to his knees, making it impossible to see where he was running. He tripped over something and rolled forward to avoid a face plant. Rocks and sticks ripped at his clothes.

Drew took a half second to glance over his shoulder before springing to his feet. Behind him and closing fast was a wall of thick fog. The barking dogs were close. He ran as fast as he could. If the fog trapped him, the tactical unit wouldn't be able to see what was going on. He'd be all alone with his backup only a few feet away.

Off in the distance, the farmhouse was lit up like a Christmas tree. The team had watched the fog roll in and wanted to make sure he could find the farmhouse if the fog surrounded him.

The dogs were so close that he could almost feel their breath on the back of his neck. His foot hit something in the fog and he stumbled. As he struggled to regain his balance, the fog wall over took him. Drew couldn't see more than a few inches in front of him. He did the only thing he could: he ran.

A sharp pain sliced at his back as something slashed at the shotgun. Drew fell forward and rolled sideways to avoid whatever hit him. He pulled the shotgun from his back and fired blindly into the fog. The sound of a dog whimpering was the only confirmation he had that the pellets had hit their target.

A second dog leapt from the fog and knocked him to the ground. He worked the pump action and fired again. He got to his feet and listened. He could hear several beasts stirring in the fog, trying to surround him.

Fear set in as he laid down fire in every direction. He hit at least three of them before a huge, wild-looking dog bit down on his left arm. For the first time, he was able to see that it was not dogs attacking him; these were wargs, just as Harriett had described them.

The shotgun went flying into the fog as he struggled to free himself from the warg's hold. He managed to pull his pistol and put two rounds in the creature's face. Another beast bit down on his right leg, lifted him off the ground and threw him. Drew fired three more rounds at the beast, sending it running.

He got to his feet and limped toward the light in the distance. The bite marks were on fire, but he forced himself to keep moving.

Out of the fog, a brown leather whip smacked across his right wrist, making him drop his pistol. He turned to see the figure of a man dressed in a leather duster and a cowboy hat standing a few feet away.

The man's whip crossed Drew's cheek, leaving a nasty cut. The whip came down again, but Drew lifted his left arm and let the whip wrap around it. He jumped toward the man. As he rolled forward, Drew pulled his silver knife from his hip and sliced upward, cutting the whip in half.

He used his momentum and attempted to tackle the man, but the man faded into the fog and Drew passed right through him. The man kicked him in the face as he landed. Drew tried to find a way to strike back, but his attempts failed as his knife hit nothing but air as once again the man's body melded with the fog.

There was a blast of light from the direction of the farmhouse, cutting right through the fog. As the light engulfed the man, he no longer looked ghostly. Drew took a chance and tackled him, hoping that without the fog aiding the stranger, he would be able to hit him.

Drew hit the man hard with his entire body, but it felt as if he were landing on a pillow. The stranger's form was soft, but solid enough to be taken to the ground. Drew put his knife to the man's throat. "It's over," he said, as he pressed the knife to the man's nearly ghostly form. "You no longer need to hunt."

The man looked up at him with blackened eyes.

"You are no slave." The ghostly sound of his voice echoed in Drew's ears.

"Slavery is over. There is no one left to hunt."

That man turned ghostly again and floated right through Drew's body. A chill shook his bones as he found himself holding a knife to the ground. He started to get to his feet as the fog began to lift. He was sure it was over and had just taken a victorious deep breath when a warg came from behind and bit down on his head.

The last thing he remembered was the sound of a rifle cracking and a sharp pain in his left temple.

# 12
# RACE AGAINST TIME

Drew found himself staring at the night sky as it flew overhead. He could feel his body moving as the jeep bounced around traffic. The sound of a horn faded off in the distance. Someone was holding his head still as the jeep whipped through the Missouri night. He could feel the bandages on his wounds, and every bump in the road sent piercing pains through his body.

"Get out of my way!" Jason yelled from the driver's seat.

"Please hurry." Pat sounded frantic as she held on to Drew's head. "You can't let him die."

"I'll make it."

"Take him to a hospital."

"The ER would take too long. This is the fastest way to get him treatment. Our camp isn't far from here and the doctor is ready to treat him as soon as we arrive."

"He's dying! Please, help him!"

The pain became too much and Drew passed out again.

When he opened his eyes, he saw Doctor Fredrick Zolmic running down the hall while pushing him on a gurney.

"Get the morphine ready on a constant drip. I don't want him to feel a thing."

Dr. Zolmic was barking orders at someone Drew couldn't see. The doctor was only five-foot six and had no real muscle tone, but he demanded command of his hospital and everyone knew better than to cross him when a life was on the line.

"Get me four pints of blood and get the damn witch in here!"

Drew felt the gurney hit the operating room's swinging doors. Pain shot through him, causing him pass out again.

Drew woke and found himself in a hospital bed. He had no idea how long he'd been out. There were bandages over his wounds and he no longer felt any pain. He sat up and saw Pat sleeping next to him. She was wearing a blood-soaked state patrol uniform. Drew's parents, Heather and Dan, were sitting on a couch on the other side of the room.

"Mom, Dad." Drew spoke in a whisper so as not to wake Pat from her sleep.

Heather jumped up and ran across the room to hug her son.

"You scared the hell out of us!" she yelled at her son.

"Keep it down. You'll wake up Pat."

"She's been at your side since you came out of the OR. She'll be mad if we don't wake her up. She seems pretty smitten with you."

"I don't think she's even eaten," Dan said.

"How long have I been out?"

"About twenty-four hours. Doc did a great job of patching you up, but you lost a lot of blood. He even asked Harriet to fix the damaged brain tissue. You'll be up and moving in no time."

"Once again, you're a hero," Heather added. "Personally, I think you're a dumb ass."

Drew chuckled. "Thanks, Mom. What happened out there?"

"You were less than a half mile from the farmhouse when the fog set in. Do you remember the fog?" Dan asked.

"I think. It came in too fast. I couldn't see a thing. I remember a pack of wargs attacking me, and there was a guy with a whip."

"They found the bodies of the wargs."

"We saw pictures," Heather said. "They are nasty-looking things, twice the size of a wolf, wild hair, and fangs bigger than my fist."

"That would be them," Drew said. "Not sure if it was the silver or just the bullets, but I was able to hold them off for a while."

"Two of our guys were hit by pellets as they tried to rush in and help," Dan informed him. "Not the brightest move. Thank God the pellets hit their body armor and bounced off without harming them."

"That's good. I couldn't live with myself if anyone had gotten hurt. What was the blast of light? It seemed to push the fog away, giving me a chance to attack the spirit."

"Harriet cast a spell and threw a ball of energy at the fog. It took a lot out of her."

Drew got a very concerned look on his face. "Oh, does Jason know?"

"He was standing right beside her when she did it."

"Sorry, Dad. I'll take care of it as soon as I'm out of here. It'll be the first thing I do."

"I know you promised to kill her if she broke the rules, but I think in this case we'll make an exception. She did save your life, after all."

"Would you feel the same way if it had been one of the others?"

"I would. Having a witch on missions may not be such a bad idea."

"Are you sure, Dad?"

"Jason, Harriet and I had a very long talk about what happened. They were both ready to leave. None of the others seemed to have a problem with what she did, and she promised only to use magic in extreme situations. She's a good person and is one of us."

"Thanks, Dad."

"No need to thank me. You're a man of your word, which is one of the things that makes you a great man. I've learned a lot from your view of the world, and maybe being a ruthless magic hunter isn't always the best thing."

Pat woke up and nearly jumped over the bed trying to hug Drew.

"You're awake!" she yelled.

To his surprise, she kissed him several times.

"I hate you for what you did, but I'm so glad you're alive," she said before nearly squeezing the life out of him with a tight hug.

"I told you it would be okay."

Pat pulled away and looked like she wanted to hit him.

"I didn't count on the fog," he admitted. "It's something we'll have to consider the next time we face a spirit."

"Next time?" she asked angrily, as if she were scolding a child.

"This is what we do. I'm not about to give it up because I had a bad fight. If I quit just because I nearly died, I would've quit years ago, and several times since."

"Do you expect me to sit here and wait for you to get killed?"

"Not at all."

"We expect you to be right beside him," Heather said.

"You want me as a hunter?"

"You risked your life for the cause, and you got the drop on one of our best hunters," Dan said. "You're already trained in firearms and self-defense. You have what it takes to join us. We'll train you and find you a position that plays to your strengths."

"What if I say no?"

"You'll make our lives very difficult. We'll have to move, and spend a lot of time making sure you don't go running around telling people about monsters. If people believe you, they'll panic. If people panic, vampires and other not-so-friendly creatures would have no reason to stay hidden. That would not be a good thing."

"You want me to give up my life and my job and live out here with you?"

"We have bases set up all over the place. You don't have to live here if you don't want," Heather said.

"But you will have to train and be ready at the drop of a hat," Drew added.

"What about money? How do you fund this operation?"

"We own several shell companies that operate with no connection to what we do," Dan explained. "Our total worth is in the billions. We pay in the high six figures, and you'll be able to retire anywhere you want. We take care of our people."

"But I have to watch Drew risk his life like he did the other day?"

"More than you'd like," Heather said, shooting her son the evil eye. "But usually he makes it out in one piece."

"Most of the time I never even get a paper cut," Drew said.

"Well, as of right now, you're officially on stand-down," Dan said.

"What? Why?"

"You have to train Pat. Besides, after watching their leader come so close to death, your team could use the R and R."

"I can't believe you are standing us down," Drew muttered.

"Train Pat, let your team take some time to rest, and you'll be back in action in no time."

"I guess you're right," Drew said with a sigh. "Let me tell the team. It'll be better coming from me."

"My hero," Heather said, kissing her son on the forehead.

# 13 STAND DOWN

Just a day after waking up, Drew was already driving the hospital staff nuts. The hospital was small with only one doctor, two nurses and a couple of volunteers. Pat made sure to be there every night with Drew, giving them plenty of time to talk and get to know everything about each other.

It didn't take them long to start having real feelings for each other. She loved Drew's passion and willingness to take great risks to help people. Drew found her fascinating and admired her courage and desire to make the world better for everyone.

Drew spent his time turning his hospital room into a mini gym. He was always running in a circle around the room, or doing pushups, jumping jacks, sit-ups or anything else he could think of to keep himself in shape. By the second day, he broke his hospital bed down and was using one of the side rails as a make shift weapon for training. The nurses enjoyed talking to him, but were happy to see him go.

He wasted no time changing out of the hospital gown. He went right to his house and changed into a pair of slacks and a polo shirt, before strapping on a gun belt with his 9mm.

As soon as he was dressed, he called for his team to gather in the briefing room. When he walked into the room, it erupted with cheers as everyone jumped to their feet. He looked over the crowd and realized it wasn't just his team: everyone in the camp was present and cheering for him.

He walked calmly to the front of the room and addressed everyone as the cheers faded.

"I'm sure you all have a lot of questions and are dying to hear what happened in the fog. It definitely was the fight of a lifetime, but first I have a few things to say."

The crowd went completely quiet.

"I was told a few of you tried to rush in to help me only to be shot for your efforts. I'm sorry for shooting you and glad no one was hurt. I must say your courage is commendable and I truly appreciate it. Everyone did a fine job considering the circumstances, and I applaud you for your efforts."

Drew started to clap, and soon the room was giving his team a standing ovation. "Next time, don't go running into gunfire without being able to see. You could've stubbed a toe." Laughter filled the room.

Drew's face got serious. He looked angry and his words matched his expression.

"As for the sniper who shot me, I'll find out who you are." Drew was not known for a hard attitude, but he'd never been shot before. "You can try to hide, but eventually the truth will come out. When I find you, I'll come for you. You and I have unfinished business. I won't rest until I shake your hand and thank you."

The tension left the room as if a person had just exhaled. The room burst into laughter. Scott Grimes stood up.

"Sorry, boss," he yelled.

"You saved my life. You drink on me for the next week."

"Thanks, boss! Rounds on me after this!" Even Drew laughed.

"The next thing on my agenda today is I want to introduce the woman who got the best of me. Pat, please stand up." Pat stood up from her spot at the back of the room. "Meet Patricia Starboard. Pat is a former Missouri Highway Patrol Officer and is now one of us." The room clapped to welcome her.

"The last thing I need to say is not meant to be a punishment in any way. My team has been ordered to stand down." There was loud protest to this news. "Our assignment is to train Pat and evaluate her skills. Once she's placed with a unit and we have all taken some well-deserved R and R, we'll be back in action. Until then, I want you all to train in your areas of expertise, but also cross-train in other areas. God knows we could use a few more of you with first aid skills, if for no other reason than to patch me up."

Drew waited for the laugher to fade.

"So now, I bet all of you probably want to know what happened."

The group responded in the affirmative. Drew spent the next hour detailing his mission and his fight in the fog. He made sure to credit everyone for the job they each did, and called out Harriet for risking everything to save him. Drew answered every question the group had for him, but he did his best to play down his own actions. Everyone already looked at him as a hero and he didn't want to build a reputation he didn't feel he deserved.

After he'd dismissed the group, he crossed the room to approach Pat.

"I guess you're my new commanding officer," she said with a smile.

"What's next, sir?"

"First, don't ever call me sir, and second, can I take you out to dinner?"

"Is there anywhere to eat around here?"

"Not really. The mess hall isn't too bad. If you'd prefer something fancier, I make a mean frozen pizza, as long as you wash it down with a lot of beer and don't mind the taste of cardboard."

"Cardboard is my favorite pizza topping."

Four months later, Drew's team was back in rotation. Pat showed great marksmanship skills and adapted quickly to the demands of being a sniper. Many of the team joked she had the perfect job to keep an eye on Drew, but no one questioned her abilities.

Within a year, Drew and Pat married. Shortly after the wedding, they announced they were expecting their first child. Harriet and Jason were also expecting, and due with their second child a month after Pat's due date. The two women became fast friends as they bonded over their pregnancies and their dangerous line of work. The two men couldn't be happier. Like most proud fathers, they just knew their kids would grow up to be best friends and the greatest hunting team ever.

# 14
# HUNTING THE HUNTERS

A few months before Pat and Drew were going to be parents, Jason's team pulled the next mission. Dan called Jason into the briefing room to review the case.

"There was a massive killing in Washington, D.C., last night. We're not clear on what happened, but five victims were found in the D.C. mall. Their throats were ripped out and they were completely drained of blood," Dan informed him.

"It's worse than that," Jason said. "According to one of my military contacts, the marine guarding the Tomb of the Unknown Soldier was killed two nights ago. His body was discovered shortly after he reported seeing someone running through the cemetery."

"It looks like we have a vampire in Arlington," Dan said.

"One that gets seen running in the graveyard where it lives, and attacks someone who will be discovered, without attempting to cover its tracks. It seems too stupid to be anything to worry about. My team will go in and get rid of it in no time," Jason replied.

"I'll make a few calls and get the place shut down for a few days. That should give you enough time to set up and clean up."

"Thanks, boss. See you in a few days." Jason had his team assembled and at the airport in less than two hours. He kissed his wife and daughter good-bye minutes before the plane took off toward D.C.

The next night, Dan burst into Drew's house. Drew and Pat heard their front door crash open and they went into survival mode. They were standing in their pajamas with their pistols aimed at the bedroom door when Dan rushed in to their room.

"What the hell, Dad?" Drew yelled, lowering his gun.

"Get the teams ready; we're going to D.C.," Dan ordered.

"What happened?" Pat asked as she covered herself with the bed sheets.

"Jason's team was wiped out, and he's the only survivor. We need to move!" Dan shouted as he ran out as fast as he'd come in.

Drew wasted little time putting on his tactical gear while Pat checked his weapons.

"I wish I was going," she admitted.

"Your job is to stay here and help the families. You're too far along to be running around chasing vampires."

"I know, my love. I still wish I was going," she said before kissing him and handed him his shotgun.

It didn't take long for every able-bodied fighter to get to the airport and help load the equipment on the planes. By the time they were ready to go, the planes were overloaded. People were sitting on boxes of hand grenades just to have a place to rest during the short flight.

Two hours later, the teams unloaded the planes in D.C. and headed toward Arlington Cemetery with a police escort. Dan and Drew drove off in a police car to meet Jason at the hospital. Dan had pulled every string he had to make sure the team had the full cooperation of the locals and the feds to conduct their investigation. The idea of hiding the team's presence never crossed anyone's mind.

Jason was barely alive. The vampire had broken several bones in his body, but it had made sure he was alive and could still talk. The doctors wrapped most of his body in a cast and stitched up the deep cuts on his face.

"Jason," Dan said as the entered the hospital room. "What the hell happened?"

"It was unbelievable, even for our standards." Jason was weak but stable. "We'd found signs of the vampire moving in and out of one specific area of the graveyard. There were only three burial vaults in that area, but we couldn't pin down which one it was sleeping in. I had the team lay out a grid of trip mines and fires to push it into a cross fire from two separate positions. I knew the vampire would avoid the open flames and if it crossed over a trip mine, the explosions would hurt. I was sure the damn thing was going to be Swiss cheese within minutes of waking up."

"I would have done the same thing," Drew said. "What went wrong?"

"Just after sundown, one of the tomb doors opened and all hell broke loose. All the fires blew out as if they were nothing more than candles on a windy day. The vampire rushed toward us, and we opened up with everything we had. He was wearing a black robe with a hood and was too fast for us. He seemed to dance around the bullets as he ran. It was like trying to shoot a shadow.

"I ordered the flamethrowers to light him up, but as soon as the flames got close, they just went out like candles on a birthday cake. Then he started throwing the team around as if they were rag dolls. He ripped us apart.

"When he got to me, he stopped. I knew I had a clear shot right into his chest, but he was too fast. He turned into a mist and my bullet passed right through. After breaking my gun in half, he wrapped me around a tree. As I lay there, helpless, he walked up and cut my face. The damn thing tasted my blood as if he were choosing a fine wine.

"He was freaky-looking. His skin was a pale white and thin enough that I could see his skull under his skin. His hands were bony-looking, like an old man's."

"Why didn't he kill you?" Dan asked.

"He said he was disappointed that I wasn't 'the hunter.' He said that I was going to live so I could tell what had happened to the others. He said he was looking for 'the bloodline of the boy.' Then I watched him rip the license plate off one of the jeeps and fly away."

"You mean he turned into a bat and flew off?" Dan asked.

"No, he just flew off as if the wind carried him."

Dan turned around and had a worried look on his face.

"What's wrong, Dad? What kind of vampire can fly without turning into a bat?" Drew asked.

"One I never really thought existed." Dan sat down in a chair. "When I was a boy, my grandfather told me the story of the first vampire, named Marcos. I thought he was just a legend meant to scare children. Considering that we learn to hunt normal childish nightmares, I thought my grandpa was just stepping it up a notch to make an impact."

"Who is this Marcos and why is he so dangerous?"

"Marcos was once a dark wizard. He was a master of the Wind Elemental powers. I don't know how he became a vampire, but he had both the powers of wind and a normal vampire. According to the story, Marcos and Von fought each other for years with neither of them able to kill the other."

"Marcos was ruthless and seemed to control the dead as well as the living. He caused the first reported zombie outbreak, along with the deaths of thousands of people over the years, but no one has reported seeing him since the time of the dragons."

"How do we kill him?"

"I don't know, but if he's looking for us, we need to protect the people we love."

"Taking a license plate won't help him. We've registered the jeeps all over the country. There's no link to our base."

"It's too big a risk. I want you to take Jason and your team. Get back to base and clear everyone out. I'll make sure Marcos doesn't return here. Once everything's cleaned up here, I'll come find you."

"Where should we go?"

"Go north to the ranch in Montana. Take nothing with you and burn the base to the ground. We can buy new equipment and rebuild when we get settled."

Drew hugged his father and said, "Good luck, Dad."

"You too, son. Keep your shotgun at the ready and don't take any risks. If something feels funny, start shooting."

Drew had Jason moved to a gurney and rolled him out to a waiting ambulance. The sun was now up, which helped him feel a bit better about the situation. When they got to the airport, the team was just arriving. They loaded up one of the planes and told the pilot to take off.

Drew knew time was short. He figured Marcos was ahead of them by at least six hours and might already be near the base. They had under twelve hours to clear out camp and be gone before Marcos attacked.

The plane made a hard landing, but Drew barely noticed. As soon as the wheels touched the ground, he jumped into the last jeep and started the engine.

"Drop the cargo door!" he ordered. Someone hit the button and the door started to drop.

"Get the plane unloaded and then blow it up. There is no place for us to land near the ranch. We can't leave anything that can be used to track us. When you're done, get to base. We move out in two hours."

Drew raced the jeep off the back of the plane before it came to a complete stop.

He arrived at the camp in a matter of minutes, much to everyone's surprise. He jumped out of the jeep barking orders.

"Everyone, pack up only the things you can't live without for a few days. Grab any pictures or evidence that says who we are."

People started to panic as they ran to their houses.

"What's going on?" Pat ran to Drew as he headed toward the hospital.

"We have to bug out, fast. Something really bad is coming. It's worse than anything we've faced before, and Dad wants us gone yesterday. Go get the camera and any pictures of us. Don't bring anything we can replace. That includes weapons and armor."

Pat kissed her husband and ran off.

When the rest of the team arrived in camp, Drew had already convinced Dr. Zolmic he would only need a large first aid kit or two. People had already started to load their belongings into jeeps and trucks, and the vehicles were gassed up and ready to go.

Drew ordered his team to double-check the camp for anything that would provide clues to their true identity. Everyone had one bag, with the only exceptions being the doctor and the cook. The only weapons allowed were those that could be concealed under a jacket or shirt. The hunters didn't like leaving their heavy weapons behind but Drew insisted.

Once everything was loaded, he ordered the caravan to head north to the ranch in Montana. He took one jeep and said he was going to stay behind and rig the camp to blow. Drew didn't want to risk any lives while setting the explosives, and assured everyone that he wouldn't be far behind.

Harriet approached him after she checked on Jason.

"I know who is coming. It's too risky for you to stay behind."

"What do you know of him?"

"Marcos dedicated his life to hunting Von. He's powerful, but has the weaknesses of any other vampire. The big difference is he's a dark wizard from the time before the war against magic. Nothing you can do will stop him."

"I'm not going to try and stop him. We can't leave anything traceable behind, so we need to destroy the camp. Once Dad catches up to us, we'll figure out how to kill him."

"At least let me offer you a protection spell. If something happens, Marcos won't be able to drink your blood without getting sick."

Drew thought about it for a second.

"Cast your spell on all of us."

"It won't be as strong over an entire group."

"We all need protection. A little is better than none."

Harriet agreed and cast her spell over the caravan. Drew felt a strange sensation in his blood. It felt like something inside of him had awakened from a lifetime of sleep.

Once the spell was complete, he ordered everyone to head out. The caravan separated into several small groups, each one taking a different route to the ranch.

Once the last of the trucks was down the road and out of sight, Drew went to work, spreading explosives and gasoline on every building in the camp. He grabbed a rifle, several magazines loaded with silver ammo, along with his shotgun, and put them in his jeep. He then took a gasoline can and made a trail of gas leading from the buildings to the edge of the road. His plan was to drive the jeep to the gasoline line, where he would stop only for a second to light the trail. He didn't even plan on staying to watch everything explode.

Drew jumped in the jeep and turned the key. Nothing happened. He tried again and again to get the jeep started but the silence of the engine told him he was a dead man.

# 15
## THERE ONCE WAS A BOY

Drew knew he didn't have enough time to hike the fifteen miles to the main road before nightfall, but he had to try. He ran to the cafeteria and found whatever food he could carry. There wasn't much left, but it would have to do.

After throwing his shotgun across his back and grabbing the rifle and ammo, he started toward the road. When he reached the end of the gasoline, he pulled a lighter from his pocket. In one small click, the camp would be toast and he would spend the rest of the day waiting for Marcos to come and kill him.

He stood over the gasoline holding the lighter for a few seconds as he considered his options. There was no way he was going to pass up the opportunity to put up a fight. Dying in battle was better than spending the entire day running to get nowhere. If he was going to die, he would do his best to take Marcos with him. He put the lighter away.

He knew the gasoline would all have evaporated by nightfall. He had to lay out a new plan and it would have to be his best plan yet. He was going to have to anticipate every move Marcos could make; if he missed even the smallest thing, Marcos might be able to escape.

Fear set in with every passing hour. He was good at hunting vampires but that wasn't going to be enough. He had to think about how a wizard—one who could control the wind—would act.

As he laid out his plan, he started to consider that he might not survive the night. Every time he tried to build in a way to keep himself safe, it only offered a way out for Marcos. He knew he was going to be in the fight of his life, and he hoped he would survive to tell his son about it one day.

The sun was about to set as Drew made the final touches to his plan. He laid several mounds of silver ammunition out around the base, and placed dynamite under each one. The dynamite was set to blow on a trigger switch tied to his hip. As soon as Drew went more than ten steps, all hell would break loose.

On top of each stack of ammo, he put a gas can, covered in garlic cloves. Since garlic was a common weapon used to kill vampires, every garden on base had lots of it. Whatever he didn't use on the gas cans, he had put on the houses, than he filled each house with more dynamite.

Drew lit a few small fires and took up a position in the center of the base. As the night sky came into view, he found himself praying Marcos wouldn't show up. All he needed to do was survive through the night, and he could make it to the main road the next day.

As each hour slowly passed, Drew found the idea of making it through the night a bit less ridiculous. He even allowed himself a bit of sleep by lying on the ground with his chin raised over his rifle. As soon as he fell into a deep enough sleep, his chin would hit the side of his gun and wake him up. He got a nice cut on his chin, but the few minutes of rest was worth it.

Around two in the morning, the night went silent. The crickets stopped chirping and the owls stopped hooting. Drew stood up and scanned the trees. He could feel Marcos watching him. He didn't know how, but he knew evil was close.

"Marcos, are you too scared to show your face?" Drew yelled out after ten minutes of silence.

"You are a brave little hunter." The voice came from the trees and sent a chill up Drew's spine. "Very stupid, but brave."

"Why don't you show yourself and face me, like you faced Von?"

"It is good that you know why I am here, but I bet you do not know why I have come for you." The voice seemed to move around the darkness.

"I don't care. I'm not going to stand by and wait for you kill me."

"Oh, I am going to kill you. First, I will tell you what I am going to do once I am done here."

"You aren't walking away from here, not if I have a say in it."

"You do not, and your little garlic trap is not going to make a difference. I have already cut every one of your lines. Did you really think I would not smell the TNT? You have a lot to learn, boy."

Drew was sure he was bluffing. He yelled, "Come on and face me, then."

Marcos was next to Drew before he could blink. A quick backhand sent Drew flying into one of the cabins. There was no explosion. Marcos wasn't bluffing about having cut the lines to the explosives. Drew picked himself up, knowing Marcos had already won.

"I have been killed thousands of times during my years," Marcos told him as he walked calmly toward Drew. The vampire was average height with a scrawny build and was more hideous than Drew had anticipated. He looked like an albino suffering from malnutrition. The only color was dried blood around his mouth from his recent kills. He looked too frail and weak to be a threat to anyone. "Each time you die, you learn a little more about yourself. I guess it is too bad for you humans that you only live once."

Drew raised his shotgun, but Marcos was no longer there.

"Face me, you coward!" Drew shouted.

"Patience, please. I have to tell you a story first." Marcos was hiding in the darkness again. "Once there was a boy who caused me great frustration. Because of him, I failed my Lord. I hunted the boy for years, but each time I tried to kill him, the boy managed to kill me. I had my chance once, but failed to finish the job. My failure was due to my desire to cause the boy pain."

Drew stood up and scanned the darkness for any signs of his enemy. The vampire's voice seemed to engulf him and every word sent a chill up his spine. Fear had taken hold of him. He had to end this.

"Enough! I don't care about how big a loser you are!" Drew called out. "Come and kill me already."

He had no idea how he was going to defeat Marcos, but he couldn't do anything if Marcos wasn't close.

Marcos attacked from his blind side, and punched Drew in the jaw. Drew dropped to the ground spitting out gobs of blood and a piece of his front tooth. By the time he looked up, Marcos was gone again.

"When a person feels pain, the taste of their blood changes. It becomes sweeter. The blood of your family is the sweetest I have ever tasted. It is so sweet that I crave it, and will be saddened when I drink the last drop from you."

"I will kill myself before I let you take pleasure in my death." Drew put his shotgun under his chin.

Marcos rushed in and stole the gun. He smashed the weapon across Drew's face before he snapped it in two like a dry twig.

Drew dropped backward to the ground, gazing at the night sky in a daze.

Marcos leaned over him, baring his fangs. "I have already killed your father after making him watch me shred his wife to pieces. You should have heard your mother scream as I ripped her legs off." He paused to watch the pain in Drew's eyes. "When I finish with you, I am going to find the rest of your little band of hunters and kill everyone one of them. Soon, everyone you know and love will beg for my mercy. Which one of your friends will scream the loudest?"

"I will kill you!" Drew struggled to speak; his pain had stolen his breath.

He pulled the pistol from his belt and fired toward one of the piles of ammo. All he needed was one lucky shot to set the entire pile ablaze. He hoped the dynamite would follow and the chain reaction would take out the entire camp.

Marcos reached out and plucked the bullet from the air, and then grabbed the pistol, crushed it, and dropped it to the ground.

"I can smell your fear and pain," he said with a demonic tone to his voice. He reached down and picked Drew up by the throat. "Can you envision me killing everyone you love? I am going to make them suffer for years before I kill them. I am going to make them watch as I torture the women and children. You know there is no sound more beautiful than hearing a mother's cries as I turn her children inside out. Have you ever seen the inside of a young child?"

Drew struggled to break free, but Marcos was too strong.

"I see your pain. I can smell it. Soon I will feast on the blood of your friends. Too bad you will not be there to watch," he said as he bit down on Drew's neck.

The bite burned as Marcos drank deep. Drew's entire body felt as if his blood was on fire, but somehow it wasn't painful. It felt as if his blood was coming to life.

Marcos dropped Drew and backed up, spitting out the blood. His skin turned green and he started to vomit.

"What kind of hell is this?" Marcos screamed as he tried to get rid of the blood.

Drew jumped at the opportunity. Harriet's protection spell had worked. Now he had to take advantage of it. He pulled his knife from his boot and stabbed Marcos in the chest. The vampire backhanded him while continuing to retch. The silver blade broke off in the creature, leaving Drew with half a knife.

The cut started to smoke, and Marcos scratched and ripped at his chest, trying to remove his the knife from under his skin. Drew had to find a weapon before the vampire recovered, but he had used all his ammo to make the trap. He only saw one option left. He sprinted to one of the fires. He burned his hand as he reached down and picked up a burning log. He held on as long as he could before throwing the log into the closest mound of ammo.

"You're not going to hurt anyone anymore!" Drew shouted as he released the log into the air.

The fire took a few seconds to light the boxes of ammunition. Marcos looked at Drew with fear in his eyes. The pile exploded as the fire reached the gas can. As the bullets started going off from the heat, more piles were hit, causing them to ignite. It took longer than planned, but soon the dynamite exploded and the entire area became a shower of silver bullets and garlic shrapnel.

# 16 HAD NO CHOICE

Pat started to worry when Drew didn't catch up to them during the trip. When news of the attack on Dan's team reached them the following day, she called the Missouri State Patrol to try to find out anything she could about the base.

As soon as she hung up the phone, Harriet asked what she'd learned. Pat broke down crying before she could get a word out. There was nothing Harriet could do but hold her friend until she was able to talk.

"There was a fire and a body found," Pat said after she calmed down. "The body was torn apart by silver bullets and burned nearly to ash by the fire and the explosions. They found a jeep with a dead battery parked near the area. They think the man was smuggling ammo and tried to cover his tracks with the fire, but after his jeep died, he was caught in the explosion."

"I'm so sorry about Drew," Harriet said hugging her friend. "He must have had no choice but to fight. If the jeep died before he could take off, he was trapped."

"Do you think he at least killed Marcos?"

"I don't know, but knowing Drew, he put up the fight of his life."

"What am I supposed to do now?"

"Jason will get better and we will continue to fight. Your job now is to protect your child. One day, you'll be able to tell him all about his brave father."

Pat put her hand on her belly, feeling the baby kick.

"If Marcos is alive, he'll be looking for us. My baby will be hunted from birth."

"We will protect you both."

"I know you'll try, but I can't raise him in this life. He needs to be safe."

"We'll support any decision you make."

"I need to bury my husband first."

"We will. We'll bury and honor them all."

"Promise me that we'll avenge them. Drew was a good man and he deserves justice."

"I promise. I'll do everything in my power to kill every vampire so our children can grow up in a world without that evil."

"My boy will. It breaks my heart, but I have to give him up. It's the only way to keep him safe. He can't know of this life. He can't ever know us."

# 17
# FROM THE ASHES

After a week-long investigation at the site of the fire, the police officers and fire investigators had all left. The explosions had done their job, leaving nothing more than a couple of burned-out buildings as the last remaining signs that the camp had ever existed.

As night fell on the area, the forest creatures crept in to explore. When the ground beneath them began to shift, the animals scurried away as fast as they could. The forest became quiet as it waited to see what secret the camp still held. The earth shifted again, and a bony, burned hand shot up from the ground, embracing the moonlight once more.

# ABOUT THE AUTHOR

Dave Rudden (1975 - still kicking) born in St Louis, MO, to a blue-collar family. He served as a United States Marine and a police officer before working his way through college to earn a computer science degree and land an engineering job. He earned two master's degrees while working full time and raising three boys with his wife, Kristy. He enjoys writing as a hobby and wants to share his stories with the world.

*Born Hunter* is the first book in the *Age of Humanity* series with many more to follow. In the world he created, dragons once ruled the earth and humans were their slaves. When the humans rose up, magic was their weapon, but it turned human against human, until it too was defeated. Now days, humans rule the world and once powerful creatures must remain hidden to avoid being hunted.

Follow Dave on Facebook as www.facebook.com/thedaverudden for story updates and future release info.

CPSIA information can be obtained at www.ICGtesting.com
Printed in the USA
LVOW08s2148130715

446052LV00026B/716/P